SCARY STORIES

THE MEDUSA DOLL

BY STEVE BREZENOFF

ILLUSTRATED BY NEIL EVANS

Raintree is an imprint of Capstone Global Library Limited, a company
incorporated in England and Wales having its registered office at 264
Banbury Road, Oxford, OX2 7DY — Registered company number: 6695582

www.raintree.co.uk
myorders@raintree.co.uk

Text © Capstone Global Library Limited 2021
The moral rights of the proprietor have been asserted.

Designed by Hilary Wacholz
Original illustrations © Capstone Global Library Limited 2021
Originated by Capstone Global Library Ltd

978 1 3982 0420 1

British Library Cataloguing in Publication Data
A full catalogue record for this book is available from the British Library.

Printed and bound in the United Kingdom

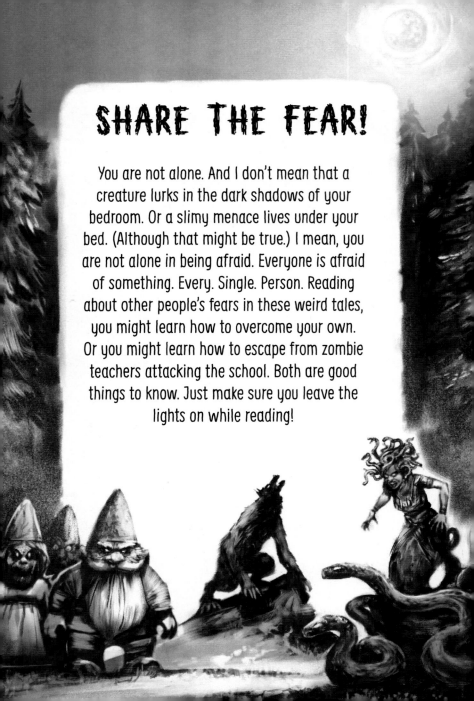

SHARE THE FEAR!

You are not alone. And I don't mean that a creature lurks in the dark shadows of your bedroom. Or a slimy menace lives under your bed. (Although that might be true.) I mean, you are not alone in being afraid. Everyone is afraid of something. Every. Single. Person. Reading about other people's fears in these weird tales, you might learn how to overcome your own. Or you might learn how to escape from zombie teachers attacking the school. Both are good things to know. Just make sure you leave the lights on while reading!

CONTENTS

Chapter 1

GIFTS

At his twelfth birthday party, Jason Argo held the plastic box firmly in his hands. The crinkly, blue wrapping paper sat in a heap at his feet.

Jason smiled as he gazed down at the face of the most powerful god of ancient Greece — as a ten-inch figurine.

"That's the last one you needed, right?" said Jason's best friend, Wilky Augustine, standing beside him. Wilky was the only other kid at the party. Everyone else was a family friend, as old as his mum. Jason hadn't even bothered inviting any other kids. He didn't have many friends. Most kids thought his interests — such as mythology and collecting figurines — were a little odd.

Jason nodded. Although Zeus was the most powerful and most famous Greek god, his figure was the hardest to find.

Wilky's gift was the last one Jason had opened. The others — all gifts from friends of his parents — lay on the floor around him. He'd been polite while opening them. But nothing meant more to Jason than his collection of Olympian gods, and finally it was complete.

"How'd you get him?" Jason asked as he used his thumbnail to snap off the clear tape that had been holding the box's top flap closed.

"It was no problem," Wilky said. He sat down on the arm of Jason's armchair. "I had alerts set up with every collector's auction site on the internet. When the Zeus figure turned up, I'd place a bid. This was actually the third one I found."

Jason looked up at him. "What happened to the other two?" he asked.

"The price went too high," Wilky replied. "Oh, and I found one other that was cheap, but it only had one arm."

Jason laughed as he rose from the chair. "Come on," he said. "Let's go and find a good spot for him on his throne with the others."

When they were halfway up the stairs, though, the front door slammed open. A woman's voice – high-pitched and a little shrill – pierced the loud hum of conversation in the house.

"Sorry I'm late!" the woman said.

Jason stopped and turned. She was a young woman with curly, wild hair. It looked as if it hadn't been brushed in ages, and it grew like the fluffy top of a dandelion. She wore a dress dotted with orange and yellow flower petals and had a smile as big as the sky.

"Aunt Amy!" Jason shouted. He hurried back downstairs and fell into her open arms.

"Late?!" Jason's mum said as she crossed the living room in two strides. She pulled her son out of her little sister's hug. "Amy, you weren't invited at all!"

Jason frowned at his mum. He loved his parents very much, but he never understood why they tried so hard to keep Aunt Amy away from him.

"Oh, Jenny," Amy said, waving her off.

"Don't be so dramatic."

Jason's mum laughed. "Me?" she said. "You're calling *me* dramatic? I'm not the one who —"

"Mum!" Jason said, interrupting her. "Not today, okay?"

Mum took a deep breath and backed off. "You're right," she said. "It's your birthday. Amy, come in and make yourself at home."

Amy flashed her teeth and set down her big tote bag. She reached inside and pulled out a parcel wrapped in newspaper.

"Happy birthday, Jason," Amy said, handing over the parcel. "I don't think you have this one."

Jason took it, surprised.

Aunt Amy hadn't remembered his birthday in years and hadn't given him a gift since the day he started school. That was when she had given him the illustrated, leather-bound book of Greek myths that introduced him to those stories.

The book had always seemed like an odd gift for a child who hadn't even learned to read yet. A few years ago, Jason had asked his mum, "Why did she give this to me?"

"Because of your name," Jason's mum had told him. "Jason was a great hero in Greek mythology."

Jason had felt proud then. Perhaps someday he'd be a great hero too. He'd read that book over and over again.

Jason looked down at the parcel from his aunt and wondered what it might be. Knowing Aunt Amy, it would probably be interesting.

"Thanks," Jason said to Aunt Amy.

Jason turned and glanced up at Mum as if

to ask, *Can I open it now?*

Mum nodded. "Go ahead, kiddo," she said. "Open it up."

Jason ran to the sofa and flopped into the cushions, the new parcel on his lap. The newspaper wrapping, he noticed now, was not a local newspaper. It wasn't even in a language he recognized.

"Where did you get this?" Jason asked.

"Oh, I can't remember," Aunt Amy said. She winked at Mum. "I'm never in one place for very long."

"Small favours," Mum said quietly.

"Well, go ahead," Wilky said. "Hurry up and open it."

Jason took a deep breath and tore off the newspaper. Beneath was a thick layer of bubble wrap.

With some difficulty, Jason pulled off
a strip of packing tape. The bubble wrap
unravelled and fell to his feet. Beneath that
was another thick layer, this one a tan, ragged
fabric, like the wrappings of a mummy.

Jason slowly unravelled it. As he did, a
fog seemed to fall over his mind. If he hadn't
been sitting, he might have fallen over.

In his hands he now held something at
once familiar and entirely unique: a figurine
like the ones he collected. It was the same size
and style, as if sculpted by the same artist.
But where those twelve gods of Olympus were
made of plastic, this one was heavy and cold.

"Is that metal?" Wilky asked. He reached
for it, but Jason moved it aside quickly.

"I think so," Jason said. He held the
figurine closer and turned it over in his hands
to examine it.

It was a woman, as sleek and lovely as Hera or even Aphrodite. But while those figures wore expressions of strength, wisdom or grace, this figure's face was twisted and angry.

Her teeth – yellow and sharp – gleamed under the living room lights. Her robe was cinched tight at the waist – not with a belt, but with a snake. And her hair – as wild as Aunt Amy's – was made of twisted snakes. They almost seemed to move as their deep-green and blood-red scales reflected the light when Jason turned her over in his hands.

Most striking, its eyes shone with red fury. Jason stared into them, and he could swear for an instant that she stared back. The fog in his mind grew denser. His breath caught in his throat as if the air in the room was suddenly as thick as mud.

Jason's blood ran cold in his veins. The muscles in his arms and legs went stiff. But at the same time, his mind felt at ease and peaceful.

Jason was happy to just let himself sink into nothingness as he stared into the figurine's fiery eyes.

Chapter 2

DISGUST

"So?" Amy said. "Do you love it?"

The sound of his aunt's voice snapped Jason out of his trance. He pulled his gaze from the figurine's eyes and nodded dumbly.

"It's amazing," Wilky said. "Medusa, right? Where'd you get it? I didn't think they even made metal ones any more."

Amy waved off his praise. "Oh, some collector in Athens," she said as she wandered into the kitchen, mumbling to herself. "Or maybe it was Crete."

"She gets stranger every year," Mum said. She followed her sister.

"Come on," Wilky said. "Let's add them to the collection."

Jason nodded again and rose slowly with Zeus in one hand and Medusa in the other. As he and his friend hurried up the stairs, the fog in his head lifted. His feet tingled with each step, as if they were waking up slowly. He shivered as his blood began to warm.

In his room, Jason's pantheon of gods had a shelf of its own. It hung over his desk. The lesser gods were already arranged there carefully. Hera, wife of Zeus, stood alone at the back. She rested one hand on the arm of a toy throne Jason had found at a car boot sale over the summer.

Jason carefully placed Zeus in the seat saved for him. The figure bent at the waist and knees as it settled into the throne. Its arms fell over the arms of the seat. One hand slowly fell on Hera's hand.

For a second, Jason was sure Hera smiled at him, happy to have Zeus at her side, where he belonged.

Jason smiled back. His whole body relaxed, and he opened his hand. He barely heard the thud at his feet as the Medusa doll hit the carpet.

"Perfect," Jason said, stepping back to enjoy the full pantheon.

Zeus and Hera were together at last. To the right of them stood tall Hephaestus, with his powerful arms. Then came twins Artemis and Apollo, Poseidon with his trident and Athena, the goddess of wisdom and courage, with a

shining helmet and a spear in one hand.

To the left of Zeus and Hera stood Hestia, the oldest and kindest of the gods. Beside her posed Ares with his feet planted and his sword drawn. Near his feet, Demeter, the goddess of the harvest, sat with her knees to one side.

Nearby, Aphrodite, the goddess of love, stood, holding an apple in one hand. Beside her was Hermes with the feathers on his ankles fluttering in a slight breeze.

"The set is complete," Jason said. He crossed his arms proudly.

"You're forgetting someone," Wilky said.

Jason squinted at him. "Who?" he said. "Oh, Dionysus? Nah, they don't make one of him. I guess they don't think kids should buy toys that drink wine."

Wilky shook his head and looked at Jason

with a crooked and confused glare. "Medusa," he said. He nodded at the floor. "Don't you remember?"

Jason looked down at the floor. There she lay at his feet.

"Oh," he said, and he bent to pick her up. "I guess I dropped her."

Jason's hand began to tingle as his fingers closed tightly around her, and an icy sweat rose between his shoulder blades.

"Yeah, I guess," Wilky said. "You ill or something? Got a fever? First you spaced out downstairs and now you're dropping precious items like they're rubbish."

Jason held Medusa in his hand and looked at her. Her wicked-looking eyes stared back. "She's not an Olympian," he said, almost spitting. "She's a Gorgon. A *monster.*"

He could hear the disgust in his own

voice. His mouth tasted sour and stale as he spoke.

"She can't go on the shelf with the others," Jason said.

"Don't you like her?" Wilky asked.

"Of course I do," Jason said. "I just —"
He stared down on the figure's twisted face.

"No," he said firmly. "I don't like her."
He turned to Wilky and held out the figure. "Here. You take her."

"You're giving her to me?" Wilky said. "But it was a birthday present from your aunt."

"I don't want her," Jason said. "You can have her. I won't tell Amy."

Wilky hesitated, then extended one hand slowly.

"Just take her," Jason said, shoving the

figure into his friend's open hand. As the cold and heavy metal left his hand, Jason immediately felt more awake, happier — as if he'd been under the Gorgon's spell and now it was lifted.

"Thanks!" Wilky said. "Hey, maybe I'll have my own cool collection soon, eh?"

"Definitely," Jason said. Wilky's mood didn't seem to change as he shoved the figure into the pocket of his baggy jeans.

Jason felt relieved. It must have been him. He just didn't like Medusa, that's all. Who would, really?

Wilky, apparently.

Chapter 3

STONE STILL

The next day was Monday, a school day. Jason waited at Wilky's locker, as he did every school-day morning. But when the first bell rang, Wilky still wasn't there.

Jason pulled out his phone and fired off a text to his best friend: *Where are you? Registration is starting!!!*

No response. Jason took one last look down the long corridor towards the main entrance. All the buses had already come and gone. Only a few stragglers hurried into the school.

Wilky wasn't one of them. Jason pocketed his phone and headed to his classroom.

* * *

As the school day ended, Wilky was still a no-show. Jason pulled out his phone and checked for messages.

"Still no reply," he muttered to himself as he got on the bus to go home. "That's really weird!"

It wasn't like Wilky. He almost never missed school. He got ill sometimes. But he always replied to texts.

Something odd was going on. Jason couldn't explain it, but a feeling deep inside still nagged at him.

When he got home, Jason didn't even put his rucksack inside. He just hopped on his bike and pedalled as fast as he could to Wilky's.

* * *

"Jason!" Wilky's mum said as she opened the front door. "I'm sorry. Wilky is ill today. He can't come out."

Jason could tell she'd been crying.

"I know, Mrs Augustine," Jason said. "He wasn't at school. I wanted to see if he was okay."

Wilky's mum began to cry again. "You're a nice boy, Jason," she said as she stepped to the side. "Come inside. Come in."

The house was full of the delicious smells of Mrs Augustine's cooking, as it always was at this time of day.

"Wilky is in bed," she said. "He has been all day!" She covered her mouth and hurried to the kitchen as her face crumbled into a sob.

Wilky's bedroom was down the hall at the back of the house. The dark hallway smelled of illness — salty and sour, but almost comforting too. The only sound was the whirring hum of a humidifier.

Jason stepped into his friend's bedroom, dimly lit and almost cloudy with vapour from the humidifier. The window on the far wall was fogged over.

Wilky lay on his bed with one thin blanket pulled up to his chest. He stared straight up at the ceiling. His chest moved up and down with slow, deep breaths.

"Hey," Jason said. He sat in the desk chair, which had been moved from the desk to the bedside. "You feeling okay?"

Wilky didn't answer. He didn't even move. He just stared unblinking, as if Jason wasn't even there.

"Hey, Wilky," Jason said. He snapped his fingers right in front of his friend's open eyes. "Anyone in there?"

"He won't answer," came a voice from behind him.

Jason turned in his chair. There stood Wilky's little sister, Pharah.

"He won't even turn his head," she said. "He's been lying there since last night. I don't think he even slept, really. Just lies there and stares. Mum's so worried."

"What's the matter with him?" Jason asked. He turned back to his friend and placed a hand on his chest. He could feel the thump of a beating heart, but it was so slow it was scary.

Pharah shook her head. "I don't know," she said. "But he sure was energetic when he got home from your birthday party yesterday."

She shrugged and walked away.

"My birthday party," Jason muttered to himself. He remembered how out of it he'd felt for a few minutes just after Aunt Amy arrived.

But he couldn't remember why. Maybe he'd been contagious. Maybe Wilky caught some horrible illness from him. . .

Then Jason saw Wilky's fist at his side, clenched tightly around a toy. His heart pounded harder in his chest.

Gently, Jason reached over and pulled Wilky's fingers open. The Medusa doll fell out and hit the floor with a thump.

Jason jumped to his feet.

"It's the doll," he thought to himself. "She has real power, just like the monster she's modelled after."

In Greek myth, the Gorgon Medusa had the power to turn mortals to stone with one glance. Wilky wasn't stone, but he looked as lifeless as a statue.

Jason looked down at the Gorgon. She lay on her back. Her red eyes shone up at him. For an instant, a fog fell over his mind and his joints went icy. He felt dizzy and slow, and wanted nothing more than to just lie down and let himself fade away like Wilky.

But then he remembered Hera's smile. It brought warmth to his cheeks. It brought strength, too, and he gritted his teeth.

"I'll take care of *you*," Jason snarled at the doll. He raised one foot and slammed it down on the figurine.

"Ow!" Nothing happened, except he'd probably have a big bruise on the bottom of his foot.

Jason kicked the doll in frustration, sending it sailing across the floor, clear under Wilky's bed and against the far wall. His toes throbbed.

"Wilky," Jason said. He dropped to his knees beside the bed. "You can wake up now. She's gone. She's not in your hand any more."

But Wilky didn't budge. His eyes stayed open and his body stayed completely still.

"I think you held her too long," Jason said. He put a hand on Wilky's arm. "Maybe you stared into her eyes. But I'll help you, mate. I promise!"

Jason got to his feet and grabbed the Medusa doll from her place against the wall. Instantly, he felt as if a cloak of ice had wrapped around his shoulders. But keeping Hera's smile in his mind, he quickly dropped the Medusa doll into his bag among his gym clothes.

Jason shouldered his bag and hurried from the room. "I'll be back, Wilky," he said. "I'll get you back to normal."

Chapter 4

THE SHOP

It was almost 5 p.m. Mum would be worried. Jason sent her a quick text before he got back on his bike: *Visited Wilky. He's ill. Home soon.*

But Jason didn't steer the bike back home. Instead, he headed into the middle of town and his favourite toy shop: Cool-ectibles.

"Jason!" the owner called out as the boy slammed through the door. The owner was Dolores Threadbare, better known as Dolly.

She'd been running the shop since long before Jason was born. "I was just about to close for the day."

"I know," Jason said. He pulled off his bag and unzipped it. "And I'm glad I caught you. This is an emergency."

Carefully, Jason used a gym sock to grab hold of the Medusa doll so his bare hands wouldn't touch it.

He placed the doll on the counter between himself and Dolly.

"That's a gym sock," Dolly said. "And it smells . . . off."

Jason pulled the sock away, revealing the iron figurine beneath.

Dolly gasped. "The Medusa doll," she whispered, her voice sounding almost scared.

"You've seen her before?" Jason asked.

Dolly looked up at him and shook her head. "Not in person," she said. "But I've seen photos . . . drawings. I've read things about her – strange things that would make your blood run cold."

"That's for sure," Jason whispered, leaning closer. "I think she has powers."

Dolly covered Medusa's face with one hand. "That's what I feared," she said. "Her eyes? Turned to stone?"

Jason quickly pulled Dolly's hand away from the doll and covered the figure with the sock.

"It's not just the eyes, not like in the myth," he said. "When it happened to me, at first I felt . . . foggy. I couldn't think straight. The next thing I knew, it was like my blood had been through a deep freeze. As long as the Medusa doll was still with me, all I wanted to do was stop everything, lie down and never move again."

"How *chilling*," Dolly said with a hint of irony in her voice.

"And my friend Wilky," Jason went on, "has been practically in a coma since this morning."

"What kind of exposure did he have to the doll?" Dolly asked.

"It was my fault," Jason replied. "I didn't like the figure. I mean, who would, after how it made me feel? But Wilky did. He didn't know. I didn't know either, really. Not yet. So I said he could have it. He must have held it all night."

Dolly sighed thoughtfully. "You saw him today?" she asked.

Jason nodded. "He won't talk or move or anything," he said. "He just lies in his bed and stares up at the ceiling. It's like he's *made* of stone, in a way."

"And where did *you* get the doll?" Dolly asked.

"My aunt gave her to me," Jason said, "at my birthday party yesterday."

"Happy birthday," Dolly said flatly.

"Thanks."

"Where did *she* get it?" Dolly asked.

"She couldn't remember," Jason said. "Somewhere in Greece, I think."

Dolly held his gaze for a moment, as if she wanted to say something.

"What?" Jason said.

"Why would your aunt give you such a dangerous gift?" Dolly said.

Jason shrugged. "I'm sure she didn't know," he said. "She probably just thought

Medusa was another harmless statue, like the ones I collect."

Dolly nodded, but she didn't seem convinced.

"Put the Gorgon back in your bag," she said, "and follow me."

Chapter 5

INDESTRUCTIBLE

Dolly led Jason through an unmarked door at the back of the shop. He followed her down a winding, dark hallway and into a small, cluttered workshop.

"Come in," Dolly said. "Welcome to my workshop." She clicked on a small lamp on a table against the far wall.

The floor and every surface – aside from a small section of the tabletop – was packed with broken toys, unmarked books, random tools and bits and pieces of computers and other electronic . . . things.

"Put her on the table," Dolly said. She dug around in a box of electronics.

Jason pulled the doll from his bag again and put her on the table. She stared up at him with her bright-red eyes. He quickly grabbed a dirty rag and covered the doll's face before her magic could get the best of him.

"If the information I've read is correct," Dolly said as she stepped up next to him, "to save Wilky – and anyone else this doll has affected – we need to destroy her."

She pulled a pair of goggles over her eyes and handed a pair to Jason. Then she raised an electric handheld rotary saw. She clicked it on and it buzzed like a screaming demon.

"I've got a special blade on it!" Dolly shouted over the saw's din. "Diamond-tipped!

Don't worry. It should make quick work of this doll!"

Jason quickly put on his goggles.

Dolly lowered the saw onto the Medusa doll's neck. Sparks flew. *SCRRREEEE!* The scream of the saw shrieked even more loudly. Soon, black smoke rose in a spiral from the saw blade.

Dolly pushed down even harder. The sparks blazed brighter. The smoke grew thicker and the room filled with the tangy smell of hot, burning metal.

"It's not working!" Dolly shouted. "I don't think the motor can . . ."

Suddenly the saw sparked, popped and switched off. As a plume of smoke rose from the saw's motor, the bulb in the lamp exploded! The workshop fell into silent darkness.

". . . take any more," Dolly finished. She pulled a penlight from her pocket, clicked it on and pointed it at the doll.

"Nothing," Jason said. "Not even so much as a scratch."

Dolly blew a frustrated breath from her nose. "I did not expect this." She slowly reached out and placed a finger on Medusa's neck. "She's not even warm."

Dolly sat down on a stool. "I'm sorry, Jason," she said. "I don't know how to destroy Medusa. I don't think I can help your friend. Or anyone else affected by her."

Jason put his head in his hands. "But it's my fault," he said. "I can't just leave him that way. I have to help him."

Dolly nodded. "I'll get on some internet forums," she said. "See what other people have done."

Dolly spun her stool round to face a small laptop. She tapped a few keys, and soon the flickering blue light of the display added a bright haze to the room.

Jason paced the workshop. He liked Dolly, but he didn't think the forums would offer a solution.

"Here's something," Dolly said. "This guy in Ukraine suggests putting the doll in a bath of acid."

Jason shook his head. "I have a feeling it won't be anything like that," he said. "She's mythical. A demigod, a Gorgon, one of the most powerful monsters in history."

"But she was mortal, right?" Dolly said.

"Yes," Jason said. He stopped pacing. "That's why Perseus was able to kill her."

"Perseus?" Dolly said. She stood up suddenly. "That rings a bell."

Dolly hurried out of the workshop. Jason grabbed Medusa with his sock-glove, shoved her into his bag and ran after Dolly. The shop owner stopped at the discount bin next to the counter.

"Look at this," she said, pulling out a figurine in a simple cardboard and plastic package. In bold print across the top it read, *Demigods of Ancient Greece*, and in smaller print beneath that: *Perseus*.

"I don't know if another doll will defeat this doll," Jason said, "but almost nothing has made sense in the last couple of days. If anyone can help, it's definitely Perseus. How much is he?" Jason reached into his pocket for his wallet.

"On the house," Dolly said, handing over the doll.

"Really?" Jason said.

Dolly tipped the discount bin so Jason could see into it.

"Oh," Jason said. The bin was full of Perseus figures. "Thanks."

"It looks like you know what needs to be done," Dolly said. "Go and save your friend!"

Jason smiled, shoved Perseus into his bag and bolted from the shop.

Chapter 6

THE HERO

Jason pedalled like mad. He knew that Perseus couldn't defeat Medusa alone, but he had an idea about who could help.

At his house, Jason leaped off the bike even before it fully stopped. He ran for the house.

"Jason!" Mum shouted as he burst in. "Where have you been? Mrs Augustine said you left her house more than an hour ago!"

"I had to make a stop," he said. He crouched just inside the hallway and pulled off his bag. "To get this."

Jason reached inside and pulled out Perseus. He tore the package open.

"A toy?" Mum said. "Jason, that is hardly a reason to . . . wait, where are you going now?"

Jason didn't answer. He bolted up the stairs and into his room. There, he placed Perseus on the shelf with the pantheon of Greek gods. As soon as Jason released his grip, the figure turned to face the gods. Then the figure dropped to one knee and bent his head.

Jason gasped and staggered backwards as a bright light began to shine. Soon he was forced to look away and cover his face with his arm. Then a great hum, like a thousand

demigods singing one long note in perfect unison, filled the room.

A second later, everything went silent and the bright light faded. Slowly, Jason uncovered his eyes and looked at the Olympian shelf.

Everything was as it had been, with all the gods in their right place. But Perseus now stood facing Jason. In one raised arm he held a shimmering sword, a gift from Zeus.

"Good thing Wilky gave me Zeus," Jason whispered to himself.

On his left arm Perseus wore a shining shield, a gift from Artemis. And on his feet, he wore Hermes' winged sandals.

As Jason had hoped, the gods had favoured Perseus, just as they did in the myth. Finally feeling hopeful, Jason grabbed Perseus and carried him down the stairs.

"Jason," Mum said, "what are you up to? What was that loud ringing noise?"

"Sorry, Mum," Jason said. "I can't explain. Just watch."

He opened his bag again and placed Perseus inside with Medusa. Then he closed the bag and waited.

Nothing happened.

"Watch what?" Mum said.

Jason stared at the bag and shook his head. "I don't know," Jason said. "Something should —"

The bag twitched. He heard something moving inside and a wet hiss-s-s-s.

"Is that a mouse?" Mum whispered, her voice quivering. She hated mice. "Or, oh no, a snake?!" She hated snakes even more.

"No," Jason said. "Listen."

Suddenly a shrill scream pierced the air. Both Jason and his mum clapped their hands over their ears to block out the sound.

Then, as quickly as it started, it stopped. The room fell silent.

Jason waited a long time, staring at the bag and feeling his mum's eyes on him. He finally kneeled down beside the bag, holding his breath.

Jason undid the zip slowly. He half expected the wicked Medusa doll to lunge out – but nothing happened.

Carefully, Jason opened the bag wide and peered inside. It was dark, but nothing moved. Slowly, he turned the bag over and let the contents fall out. First came a pile of dirty gym clothes.

"Oh, Jason," Mum said, disgusted. "How long have those been in there?"

He shook the bag again, and Perseus fell out and hit the floor with a thud. The mythical hero now wore his sword in its scabbard on his belt and his shield on his back. In his hand, he held a sack.

"Ewww!" Jason said quietly. "That must be Medusa's head."

As for Medusa, aside from her head in a sack, she seemed to have vanished. Jason put the bag down.

"That's that, I guess," he said, almost sad the adventure was over, and even that his gift from Aunt Amy was gone forever.

But the bag shook again and then fluttered around the floor, before finally rising up into the air with the sound of flapping wings.

"What's it doing?" Mum shouted. "Are you keeping a pet bird in there too?"

Jason shrugged. He grabbed the bag out of

the air and the flapping stopped.

Jason reached into the bag, his heart thumping against his chest. In the otherwise empty bag, his hand quickly found something new. He wrapped his fingers around it and pulled it out.

It was Pegasus, the white, winged horse. The figurine stood on its hind legs with its head high and its huge, majestic wings spread wide.

"Of course," Jason whispered. "The last gift to Perseus. Pegasus was born out of Medusa's neck after Perseus defeated her."

Jason didn't feel around in the bag any further. He knew Medusa was gone, with only her head and Pegasus as proof she'd ever been there.

Chapter 7

THE REAL GIFT

"I suppose I won't believe you when you explain all this," Mum said.

"Probably not," Jason said.

"Then don't bother," Mum said, shaking her head. She walked into the kitchen, dazed.

Jason pulled out his phone and called Wilky's house. While he waited for someone to answer, he admired Pegasus. The famous flying horse would be the new stand-out in his collection, magnificent not just for being a beautiful horse, but for the story it told about this adventure as well.

"Hello?" came a troubled voice through the phone.

"Mrs Augustine?" he said. "Is Wilky feeling better?"

"No," said Wilky's mum. "He's —"

In the background, Jason heard Wilky's confused and scratchy voice. "Mum? What's going on?"

"Wilky!" Mrs Augustine screamed with joy. "You're awake!"

"Tell him I'll see him tomorrow, Mrs A.," Jason said. He hung up.

Jason walked into the kitchen.

"Mum," he said, "is Aunt Amy still in town? I have to ask her —"

The doorbell rang, and Mum and Jason ran to the front door. Jason pulled it open.

"Ah," said Aunt Amy. She stood on the front step in her wide-brim hat, pulled down to contain her wild hair. Her suitcase, beaten and taped, sat at her feet.

Amy spotted Pegasus in Jason's hand.

"So you worked it out," she said with a smile. "I knew you would. Well done." She leaned closer and said quietly, "You've had that book of Greek myths since you started school, after all. You must have had time to read it once or twice."

"You — you knew?" Jason said, stunned. "About the Medusa doll?"

"Of course!" Aunt Amy said, chuckling and patting him on the arm. "That's why it was so clumsily and thickly wrapped. Tricky stuff. But there's no other way to get the

Pegasus figurine, you know. And I knew you'd want a collection to be proud of."

Eyes wide, Jason opened his mouth to speak, but nothing came out.

"Perfect," Amy said. "Goodbye, Jenny," she added, turning to Jason's mother. "When I find another treasure, I'll be back."

"*Please* don't," said Jason's mum.

Aunt Amy turned and left. Mum closed the door.

"Did *you* know?" Jason asked his mum.

"About Medusa or whoever?" Mum asked. She shook her head. "No. But about my sister and the . . . unusual gifts she tends to give? Of course."

Mum sighed and almost seemed to smile, as if a faraway memory was bubbling in her mind. "How about I tell you the story of my thirteenth birthday," she said, heading back to the kitchen, "when ten-year-old Amy gave me a wreath of garlic, a bottle of holy water and a wooden stake."

"Whoa," Jason said, and he hurried after his mother to hear the tale.

ABOUT THE AUTHOR

Steve Brezenoff is the author of more than 50 chapter books, including the Field Trip Mysteries series, the Ravens Pass series of thrillers and the Return to the Titanic series. He has also written three young adult novels, *Guy in Real Life*; *Brooklyn, Burning*; and *The Absolute Value of –1*. In his spare time, Steve enjoys video games, cycling and cooking. He lives in Minneapolis, USA, with his wife, Beth, and their son and daughter.

ABOUT THE ILLUSTRATOR

Neil Evans is a Welsh illustrator. A lifelong comic art fan, he drifted into children's illustration at art college and has since done plenty of both. He enjoyed a few years as a member of various unheard-of indie rock bands (and as a maker of bizarre small press comics) before settling down to get serious about making a living from illustration. He loves depicting emotion, expression and body language, and he loves inventing unusual creatures and places. When not hunched over a graphics tablet, he can usually be found hunched over a guitar or dreaming up book pitches and silly songs with his partner, Susannah. They live together in North Wales.

GLOSSARY

coma state of deep unconsciousness from which it is very hard to wake up

energetic strong and active

exposure length of time someone is left without protection from something harmful

Gorgon mythical monster with snakes for hair that could turn people who looked at them to stone

humidifier machine that makes the air in a room moist

mortal human; referring to a being who will eventually die

mythology old or ancient stories told again and again that help connect people with their past

pantheon collection or group of gods

scabbard case that holds a sword or dagger when not in use

unison say, sing or do something together

TALK ABOUT IT

1. Jason's mum isn't happy when her sister shows up at the birthday party. Why doesn't she want Aunt Amy there? What is she afraid her sister might do?

2. When Jason realizes the Medusa doll might be putting a spell on him, he gives it to his best friend, Wilky. Why would he do that? What would you do in his situation?

3. Jason uses the Perseus figure to defeat the Medusa doll. Why did he need that figure when he had twelve other Greek god figures in his collection? Why couldn't any of the other figures defeat the Medusa doll on their own?

WRITE ABOUT IT

1. We don't get to see what happens to Wilky after Jason gives him the Medusa doll. Write a new chapter that describes how the doll affects him and explains how he ends up in a coma-like state.

2. What is the creepiest or scariest toy you've ever seen or received as a gift? Draw a picture of it and write a paragraph explaining why it was so scary. If you haven't had a creepy or scary toy, imagine one and draw and write about it.

3. Jason's aunt has a habit of giving mysterious — if not slightly sinister — gifts. What might she give Jason for his thirteenth birthday? Write a short story that details Jason's next spooky adventure.